T.M. Cooks is the pen name of the following collaborative writing team. The contributors are:

- Ivo Parkes

- Paignton Smith

- Simon Taylor

- Ellie McPhilbin

- Israar Nazir

with cover design by Richard Seymour. The project was overseen by Joe Reddington, Dr Yvonne Skipper and Richard Seymour.

The group cheerfully acknowledges the wonderful help given by:

- Baljinder Bains

- Jennie Launchbury

- Emma Windess

- Nicola Harrison

- Thalia Mountney

- Joanne Aubrey

- Emma Ikoku

- Rebecca Molloy

And a big thank you goes to Higher Horizons+ who funded this wonderful project.

It's been a wonderful opportunity, and everyone involved has been filled with incredible knowledge and enthusiasm.

Finally, we would like to thank all staff at Burton and South Derbyshire College for their support in releasing our novelists from lessons for a full week.

The group started to plan out their novel at 9.15 on Monday 30th April 2018 and completed their last proof reading at 12.00 on Friday 4th May 2018.

We are incredibly proud to state that every word of the story, every idea, every chapter and yes, every mistake, is entirely their own work. No teachers, parents or other students touched a single key during this process, and we would ask readers to keep this in mind.

We are sure you will agree that this is an incredible achievement. It has been a true delight and privilege to see this group of young people turn into professional novelists in front of our very eyes.

Flashback

T. M. Cooks

Contents

1

Chapter 1

A Day In Paradise

As the sun started to loom over the

horizon, the birds started to sing their cheerful whistling song, but in one certain dark and gloomy house a young man awakens from a frightening nightmare about his childhood and the time he was abused by their father, how his mother had sadly passed when he was the age of three.

The young man then noticed that his precious treasure is no longer in the bed with him, feeling shocked and still frightened the young man looked top to bottom to find out where the love of his life had gone to even though part of him knew that she'd probably just gone out working or went to the shop.

After having an episode of self doubt and recovering from a nightmare which no human should ever face, he decides it's time to get ready and to take a look downstairs to see if his darling was there. While he got ready a note fell out of his pocket which said "Hi Jordan, not home currently, love Ana".

Jordan put the note on the side and started to wonder where exactly has Ana gone too and why was it placed in his coat pocket. Jordan continued to get ready but then started to have a small panic attack, so he rushed to the bedside table and took a bunch of his tablets in hopes to calm his nerves and once he was fairly calm Jordan tried to carry on getting ready.

It just hit 8 AM and Jordan was down stairs in the kitchen making himself some breakfast, he was still concerned about Ana's whereabouts and wondered what she was up to. Jordan knew that Ana wasn't at work till 1 PM and he began to realise how

unusual this was of Ana. Jordan then re-
alised that the people in his neighborhood
knew that Ana used to be a big cheater
and a player which left him there questioning himself.

With Jordan's panic attacks not set-
tling he decided to get some alcohol out
of the fridge even though his doctor had
strictly told him to avoid any alcohol at
all costs. After having two bottles of alcohol Jordans nerves had fully come down
but has been replaced with serious confusion and self doubt but still managed to
finish making his breakfast.

While he started to play his favorite ra-
dio station, Jordan found Ana's phone on
the side of the table. He thought that she
might of just forgotten it or was in a rush
so Jordan laid it down on the side of the

table near where he was eating his breakfast.

Jordan started to hear a heavy bling
sound which was coming from Ana's phone
which at first he decided to ignore as he
believed it was private but then started to
hear it again and again, he then slammed
the plate down in the kitchen sink and felt
it was time to investigate what all the fuss
was about.

In a shocking sight Jordan found at least
ten notifications from the same person named
Eric. In the effect had made Jordan shell
shocked and very suspicious so he proceeded
to unlock her phone to investigate the messages.

What he found had made him feel very
angry and scared that he was losing his
number one, a text stood out which he

read out loudly, it said "Hi Eric, let's meet today in the park or something and we can well you know. I'll be there at 9:30 AM. Hope to see you there ;)"

After reading the text Jordan furiously slammed the phone to the ground cracking the top right corner of the screen, then picked up his favorite chair and smashed his TV with it. With glass everywhere all over the floor Jordan still continued to punch everything he could find, then rushed to get more alcohol until he could no longer stand.

Chapter 2

Spark That
Ignites the Way

As the day begins, Mac starts flowing

into his daily routine which is looking through any notes he has on any leading stories that he's been working on so he begins to look through his drawers and compartments which turns up empty so then he starts to look at his computer to see if he has any programs opened up to just remind himself if he's been working on any pieces lately and he notices that he hasn't worked on anything at all in a week's time, so he proceeds to just slump in his chair and he starts to let his mind drift slowly away so he can think of something to do.

While Mac is daydreaming he starts to think about why hasn't his career picked up and it starts to bother him since he's following everything he's been taught to do throughout his career, he followed everything what he was taught and it's annoying him that he's getting nowhere since every story he has written hasn't gone down well, it either gets negative views or people just don't even read the pieces he produces since no one wants to hear about anything too normal as they all want thrilling pieces of about how trekking through a jungle or adventuring into an abandoned building to look for anything of the unnatural not of fluff pieces of how the weather is going to get worse through the entirety of a month.

Mac starts to dream about his perfect piece which will ignite his career into getting popularity and riches from just doing what he loves and begins to wonder if he will ever encounter anything which will completely change his life at all, like reporting a history making event or encountering anything crazy along the lines of time traveling. All of these things would be lovely to be able to report on but knowing his luck it would never happen due to how everyone despises his work which gets published onto his website. Which this causes him to snap back into reality and look at the time and wonder what he's actually done today at all besides self-loathing.

Chapter 3

Downfall of The Star

With broken alcohol bottles scattered

15

around the floor, the place looking like a bomb went off, Jordan began to wake up but felt like a completely different person. A type of person who was careless and doesn't care about anything, that he hated his life and didn't want to live anymore because he knew that he lost the most important thing to him which was Ana.

He kept second guessing himself and started to have a major panic attack which this time Jordan flushed his tablets down the toilet and decided to go out for a walk to attempt to clear his head.

Twenty minutes later Jordan found a royal casino with flashing lights, even though he made a promise to Ana that he'd stop going to casinos and will pack in gambling he decided to break that promise as he feels Ana has done the same thing about never leaving him.

Forty minutes had passed and Jordan had lost three games which lead to him losing a lot of money which was needed for his football team. Still feeling careless he decided to stay for a few more games which later lead to him losing all his money.

Unexpectedly one of Jordans old friends turned up and asked Jordan if he was up for a drinking contest, even though Jordan knew that the friend was unaware of his illness and the impact that the alcohol could have on him, which he then decided to accept the challenge.

After sixteen bottles of alcohol both Jordan and his friend were both completely out of it, unaware what was going on but they proceed to dance on the tables, bar chairs and dance floor while slowly stripping off. Unaware of what was going on one of the guests recorded this event and decided to post it to the internet. Which after this Jordan called a taxi to take him home as he could no longer stand up. A few minutes later Joran arrived home to what looked like an empty and abandoned house to have a few minutes sleep so he could try to recover.

Chapter 4

Engineer's Ambition

After waking up from a nightmare which

Jason experienced, he then looks at the alarm clock realising he's late for work. The alarm clock reads out it's approximately 8:50am he only has 10 minutes to get ready and get to work. Luckily enough for Jason, his work is only around the corner from his house, so he starts to get ready. Jason remembers that everything he needs for work is actually ready for him on the kitchen table as he organised his stuff last night. Jason rushes towards the kitchen table whilst opening his hands clenching his tools as if they were the most precious tools on earth. Jason then leaves his house and starts to walk rapidly towards his work place, looking at his watch it states the time is 8:55 am, he decides to stop at the shop to order himself a detox drink so he can start the day.

After Jason ordered his detox, he waits for the shop staff to make it and prepares his money to purchase it. Costing him 5, he looks in his wallet realising he has only got 10 notes and no 5 notes. After realising Jason then snatches out the 10 note from his wallet and passes the money to the member of staff. He then receives his change back, laughing grabbing his 5 change and keeps it safe in his wallet, protecting it with his life so that he can use it for the next time he returns to buy a drink. After the completion of the purchase he then receives his drink and walks back out of the shop heading towards his final destination, his workplace.

Jason, who is 6'6ft tall, closes in to his workplace and finishes his drink to then throw it in the bin. After drinking, Jason feels refreshed and energetic to work for hours. Jason arrives at work, as he grabs his key out to open the gate, he gets a reminder from his phone stating " today the machine needs updating." He opens the gate and walks in to his workplace opening the main door. Jason walks to his flashback machine and hears a noise " beep beep beep" Jason realises the machine is overheating as it was left on, quickly rushes towards the machine. With physical power Jason pushes the big red button to turn the machine off. He feels relieved. Jason remembers in his nightmare that this exact moment occurred. In shock he then sits down to cool himself as his face was covered with redness all around, as if to say someone had just painted his face red.

Whilst Jason is sitting down, he tries

to forget about the incident and begins to think of ideas on how to improve his flashback machine. Jason climbs to the top of the stairs directing him to his equipment which he then grabs a piece of paper and black pen, then slides down the stairs and sits at his work desk. Jason begins to jot down his ideas on his piece of paper in a old fashioned way, drawing a spider diagram. Jason begins to plan using his ideas on how to improve his flashback machine.

After a hard work of pulling ideas from his head, Jason finally completes his planning and begins to modify his flashback machine. Jason's flashback machine begins to come back alive, after he switches on the button to power it. Once it had been powered back to alive again, Jason lifts the flashback machine with his magnetic hands beginning to scan the entire machine with his eyes. Jason notices that the battery of the machine is about to die out. He then grips the electric wire with his sharp claws plugging it in to the battery and then powers it. After reviving the machine, Jason finally takes a break to get his breath back.

Chapter 5

Fall from Grace

What once was a bright and lovely day had a drastic change when the next day arrived. The sky looked as if the clouds was floating over the floor. The wind was furiously blowing across the land and the rain quickly turned into hail which seemed as if the sky was throwing heavy rocks.

Jordan then proceeds to wake up

He doesn't remember anything from last night but still feels aggressive and angry, all he wants to do is just walk into the street and beat someone up for no reason at all. Jordan feels hurt, used and feels his life is worthless, but says to himself he still has the football team so he hopes things will get better over time.

Jordan realises he has a text from the manager, he decides to leave it for a bit because he feels it's only a minor thing about team updates and the next positions, so he proceeds to get himself a hot chocolate and relax on the sofa for a bit.

After twelve minutes Jordan checks his phone to see a massive shock, one of his biggest nightmares has come true

In fear and shock Jordan starts to cry, his teardrops fell like heavy rain on a tragic and emotional event. He proceeds to read the message out loud "due to the video that was published last night on social media, I can no longer accept you on the team which means we no longer require your service. This is a tough decision but it had to be made."

In a furious mood, Jordan slams his phone on the floor, instantly cracking the screen then proceeds to get some more alcohol out of the fridge. He decides to attempt to chill out, in hope that the nightmare will soon be over. But he picks up his phone and finds a news article with his face on it.

Then Jordan says to himself, "this night-mare is only getting worse"...

The news article headline reads "Drunken fool is fired from the team", in shock Jordan proceeds to watch the video which has lead to him hating himself and wonders how stupid can he be. Quickly Jordan finds a knife and thinks about ending it all but has a better idea to try and find where Ana the cheater has gone off to...

Chapter 6

Breaking Point

Ana is excited about going to the beach with Jordan she thinks to herself it will make her feel less guilty about having an affair with someone else behind his back. She meets up with Jordan and greets him with a hug and a kiss to the cheek. "Hi babe, everything okay?" Jordan just stands there and smiles at Ana taking her hand and started heading towards the beach. Ana tries talking to Jordan just to make casual conversation as they walk to the beach, but Jordan just ignores what she says and carries on walking. Ana gives up trying to talk to him and starts texting her friends trying to arrange a girls night out sometime next week when no one is busy. Ana suddenly giggles at a message that she receives and this makes Jordan jealous and he looks over her shoulder and begins to read the message and Ana's reply. Ana notices that Jordan is reading her messages over her shoulder and begins to get defencive and starts asking him questions about that he has no trust for her and he is invading her privacy. Jordan covers up that he is mad at her and says "I only wanted to see what was making you happy that's all." Ana apologies for jumping to conclusions and goes back to looking at her phone.

Jordan and Ana reach the beach. Jordan begins to get anxious and nervous about confronting Ana about the affair. Jordan finds the courage and his voice and asks Ana "Ana there's something I need to ask you and I want you to be truthful honest with me" Ana turns to Jordan and smiles at him and asks "sure what's on your mind?" Jordan doesn't hesitate and asks "Ana.. are you having an affair with another man?" Ana is surprised. She begins to question herself and asks herself "Was she not as careful as she thought?"

"How did Jordan find out?" "Did Jordan catch her in the act?" "Is that why he brought her to the beach?" "What was he going to do?" Ana didn't know what she should say to him so she started to think of something to say that would sound convincing to Jordan, but nothing was coming to mind. So Ana decided to just wing it and hope for the best.

"Jordan I would never do such a thing to you, I love you. Why would you think I would do such a thing. You know how much I love you and would do anything to stay with you and would do anything to keep you. Why would you say such a thing you are my everything and I don't want to lose you." Jordan knew she didn't care about him as much as she was making out she did, and that everything she was saying was complete lies. Jordan couldn't take no more of her lies.

Jordan starts screaming at Ana and getting all up in her face, "YOU ARE JUST FULL OF LIES!!" ' I KNOW YOU HAVE BEEN SEEING SOMEONE ELSE BEHIND MY BACK!! I HAVE SEEN THE MESSAGES ANA, I HAVE READ THE MESSAGES ANA, DON'T LIE TO ME!!" Ana freezes to the spot and just looks at Jordan expressionless. She doesn't know what to say to him or do so he would calm down a bit.

Jordan starts moving towards Ana causing her to move further back closer and closer to the edge of the cliff. Ana finds her voice and continues to argue with Jordan saying that the messages were a joke they weren't what he thought they were

about and that he should believe her she
was his girlfriend. Jordan couldn't take no
more and pushed Ana hard. Ana stumbled backwards, lost her balance and fell
over the cliff side. Ana screamed. Then
silence Jordan stood watching her fall and
watched her as she disappeared into the
sea below. When Ana was not to be seen
he turned and walked away, heading back
down the beach in the direction which he
and Ana had just walked just moments before. Smiling.

Chapter 7

The Search Party

On a dark, windy morning with the clouds looking as if they are floating along the surface the group of friends decide to form up a mini-search party to look for Ana. They had asked Jordan where he last saw her and with a stuttering voice he said "I last saw her at home but am sure she's gone to the cliffs over in the distance as she loves to go there when she's upset."

The friends pick up their pace and like a lightning bolt they ran to the cliff area in hopes that they'll find Ana sitting there but once they arrived all they found was a misty, dark, silent cliffs with a drop that looks like a straight ticket to the world below.

With tears of failure falling slowly down the group of friends eyes, they decide not to lose any hope. They decide to search the area top to bottom anxiously hoping they'll see their lovely friend once more, once the group splits up to search Natasha decides to question Jordan to see if there was any links to do with Ana's disappearance.

Natasha decides to ask Jordan basic questions while paying close attention to Jordan's face reactions to see whether he is telling the truth or not, she asks him basic questions such as "was there any arguments before she vanished" "what was she doing the night before and did anything weird happen or stuff out of the usual". In hopes to get an answer Natasha keeps asking and asking before Jordan has any time to really respond.

Trying to stop his hand from shaking and making any suspicious movements Jordan says "no, there wasn't. I mean there was nothing out of the usual. I just. I just want her back.. please please help me get her back". Natasha seems a little suspicious about Jordan's response but doesn't take it on board as she thinks his just upset and confused why she would go.

When Natasha looks away Jordan throws a cheeky, evil grin because he knows that he's just gotten away with it and feeling confident in himself he says to the group "it's a waste of time searching here, she's probably just gone to the park or something".

With Jordan sending the group on a wild goose chase they decide it would be wise to look around the park incase she had gotten lost there. With hopes tumbling and the weather getting miserable the group arrives at the park.

They split into groups, they search the park top to bottom, they ask people who are at the part but there is still no luck. There is no sign of Ana and no one knows her whereabouts nor do they really care or seem interested, Jordan tries to persuade the group it's getting late and she's probably just camping in the woods or something, that it'd be wise to pick up the search the next day.

With hopes beginning to fade the group decide to call it a day and to pick up search the next day, they try to come up with ideas like missing posters but Jordan trying to act wise says "that'll be a waste of time, no one will read them" so the group scraps that idea and plan to meet up the following day.

Chapter 8

The Awakening

Ana begins to wake up. She is confused as she does not recognise where she is. The last thing she remembers is walking along the beach, arguing with Jordan and then her falling backwards. Then complete darkness. Ana starts asking herself questions. "Did he really push me?" "Why would he do that?" "Am I dreaming?" "Where am I?" After a moment of thinking Ana got up off the bed in which she was lay on and walked over to the window and looked out. Ana didn't recognise where she was there was people in the street but no one who she knew and they were all dressed in strange clothes. Ana then looks at herself in the mirror and notices she is wearing strange clothes too. She began to think "These aren't my clothes, where are my designer jeans and top?" "Where is my phone?!" Ana began looking frantically for her phone but she could not find it anywhere. She eventually gave up looking and sat down and began to cry. She was lost. She had lost everything.

After awhile of crying, Ana decided to pull herself together and take in her surroundings to try and figure out where she was and how she got here. She begins looking around the house looking for any clues which can tell her where she is. All she can find in the closet is laced corsets and long silk puffy dresses. Clothes that she would always say she would never wear as it would make her look fat. She then moved onto the rooms downstairs looking through draws and cupboards. The first thing she thought was "Where's all the food?" The strange house had no food in there whatsoever. But that didn't stop her from finding out where she was. Ana opened a draw in a old looking dresser and found some newspaper clippings. Year 3rd June 1837. Ana kept on repeating the year in her mind. "1837.1837.1837." The year 1837 sounded familiar to Ana but she couldn't quite remember why.

Then it hit Ana. She remembered why that year sounded so familiar to her. Back in high school she did a whole project on the Victorian era. The Victorian era being in the year 1837. Now everything began to make sense to Ana, the strange house, strange clothes, the strange people she seen outside the window. She was in the Victorian era. Ana begins to get upset again, the realisation that she wasn't going to see her family and friends again hurt her too much to think about. Ana buried her face into the pillows and sobbed until there was no more tears left to cry. Af-

ter Ana had calmed down she began to let
her new life sink in. she started to think
about the fresh start she had been given
away from all the cheating and lying and
arguments. The more she thought about
it the more she began to feel happy and
get use to the idea of her starting a new
life in a whole new era. Ana went looking
for some shoes to put on and something
that would keep her warm as it look very
windy and cold outside.

Ana hesitantly opens the door and is
soon greeted by the thick smoky air along
with the hustle and bustle of people in the
streets. Ana stepped out onto the streets
nervous and unsure of which direction she
should go. The strange people rushing around
in front of her seemed friendly enough. For
a good few moments Ana stood frozen to

45

the spot and just watched on to the chaos which was happening before her. She soon found the courage and started walking about familiarising herself with the different stalls and shops which are around her, not leaving the street she was on so she didn't lose the house she came out of. The more Ana walked and took in her surroundings she began to feel more comfortable and felt like she was beginning to fit in with everyone else.

After a while exploring the outside world Ana decided she should start heading back 'home" before it got too dark or something bad happened. Ana turned swiftly to head back down the high street the way she came accidently bumping into a young man knocking him down. Ana quickly started apologising and helped him to his feet. "I'm ever so sorry I didn't see you, I'm new around here I'm not familiar with where I am, please forgive me sir." The young man just laughed and said it was okay he wasn't hurt or anything. Ana let go of the man's arm and looked

him in the face. Ana was left speechless, she just stood there and stared at the man stood in front of her. "I'm George, and your name would be?" the tall man asked. Ana snapped back into reality and stuttered her name back. "A..A..A..Ana." Ana started blushing and began thinking about how attractive he was.

Chapter 9

Work in Progress

With the sound of an old rusty hammer banging across a shiny metal surface, Jason is working on a machine which can view the past, view the time events of History. He calls it the Flashbacker 2000, while working on the wiring he suddenly shocks himself three times "Damm thing" he screams.

When the wiring is finished and fully working he celebrates with a gentle pack on the back from himself, smirking and grinning Jason decides to take a short break to recuperate from all the technical work that he's been doing. So he decides to head on over to the fridge and get himself some hot chocolate drink.

After serving up the drink for himself Jason raises his glass and says "this one's for you papa, I hope to see flashbacks of you soon. I love you and miss you so much". Once having a quick gulp of his delicious drink Jason decides to check in with the news to see what's happening in the world.

A story about the city's currency is the first thing to be discussed, then the police cuts and how an ape was killed in a zoo for carrying a little boy around in the exhibit area trying to protect it from any harm that could occur. Then out of nowhere a broadcast shows saying "Missing girl named Ana, possibly dead and no traces of where she's gone to or who was the last to see her" this causes Jason to spit out his drink all over the floor and in shock carries on watching the news and updates about Ana's disappearance.

As the tears start to fall down Jason's eyes he carries on repeating himself "why why would someone do that to a lovely girl like that what's wrong with this planet.", puzzled and confused Jason carries on listening to what's being said, the news presenter has said "the Police have investigated her last known location to only find nothing, if you see her please contact the Police straight away or go to her boyfriend Jordan. My hearts and prayers go to Ana and her family on this horrible day".

Jason throws the hot chocolate away and decides to have a beer to try and calm himself down after hearing the sad news about his beloved friend. He keeps questioning himself why and starts to blame himself for not being there for her as she was always there for him. But he does not give up hope so he decides to pull out his whiteboard and grabs a board pen.

With the tears constantly running down his sad and lonely face, Jordan tries to put together who was the last person to see her and who her friends was. He tries to put faces to names and gather up clues about the sudden disappearance of Ana, with load of results to dead ends Jason decides not to give up but throws away the pen and sits down with his head in his hands crying for mercy and prays that Ana is alright.

Chapter 10

Breakthrough

After Mac finishes moping about he decides he will head down to the store to get
a drink and while he's out to get some fresh

air, so Mac goes to grab his coat and begin to walk out the door leaving behind his office in a complete state like a bomb went off so he left his office and Mac begins to wonder if he will find anything what will be worthy of writing about to publish onto his website since he needs to get something out otherwise he will not have published for two weeks if he doesn't get anything out now.

While Mac is walking down to the store, hoping to find something to write about while on his travels to the shop he begins to ponder about how he needs to sort through his drawers and compartments to get rid of any old notes and stories that he tried to publish but just wasn't juicy enough for anyone to be interested in to reading about. Mac also starts to wonder about type of drink he is going to get. Maybe something tangy to perk himself up to motivate himself into doing more research into looking for more stories so he can finally publish something onto his website and get back into his mojo.

During his walk he notices a group near the store he goes to chatting about something so Mac decides to slow his pace down a little so he can overhears their chatter and the first word he hears is "disappearance of a girl called Ana" and this intrigues Mac so he slows his pace even more to overhear more of the group chatting away. He finds out more information regarding about it and he hopes that his will be the breakthrough he needs to get his career back on the track to becoming a successful journalist and this will be the piece will do it for him.

As Mac basically comes to a grinding halt he spots one of the group members looking his way and he decides to call them over to ask about this disappearance and a girl walks over to him and she begins to ask "what he wants" and mac replies "I'm a journalist and I'm wondering who's this girl who has disappeared" and the girl replies "oh it's a friend of mine Ana her name is oh and my name is also Natasha" Mac replies "oh well my name is Mac and I'm sorry to hear about your loss, was there anything out the ordinary before she disappeared" Natasha Responds " not has a I know of since she was always focused on doing what's best for to keep on top of her career" Mac responds " is it possible for me to have a picture of her to put her on my website to give her some publicity to see if more people will search for her" Natasha replies " yeah sure" Natasha ask for Mac's email and proceeds to send mac a photo of Ana

Mac gets the notification of the email containing the picture of Ana has come through and he notices the time and he says "oh damn I've took longer than I expected on my break" and proceeds to thank Natasha for her telling him about Ana's disappearance and just as Mac is leaving he asks to take Natasha's number which she gives to him so he can call her if he finds any discoveries relating to Ana's Disappearance. Mac proceeds to the store and grabs a drink randomly from the fridges within the store and he quickly pays for the drink and proceeds to walk back to his office with this disappearance story in his head and how he's going to write it so he can publish it to get more people looking for her.

Chapter 11

The Construct of Success

Passing through hours of hard work, Jason begins to feel fatigue and takes a break to catch his breath back. In the process of catching his breath back, Jason starts to listen to some of his favourite artists to feel relaxed. As the room filled with voices, Jason starts to think about Ana's death. Feeling sorrow for Ana, Jason begins to glance at his flashback machine. The flashback machine starts to call him. "Bang" a pen falls from the machine landing towards Jason. After a sign from the machine calling him, Jason answers the machine realising that he can actually help out how Ana's death occurred.

However Jason begins to feel blessed as he knows that his flashback machine has been telling him all this time that he can use it to help find out, which then brings a tear of happiness to his eyes. Jason also knows that this is a big chance for him to get the word out that his flashback machine exists and is really alive. As Jason wipes his tears gently, he looks at his flashback machine as if they were destined to be together. Jason then reaches out on the floor picking up the pen and putting it back in its place which then he begins...

Jason's flashback machine becomes steady as Jason changes its setting. Jason had left the machine on no memory setting which he then changes it to flashback memory only. The flashback machine begins to make creepy noises as it prepares to change settings. Jason rushes towards the end of the flashback machine with the big black and bold sign "safe shield" catching his eyes, he quickly presses the button to activate it.

With emotions running all over the place, Jason starts to put the flashback machine in self cleaning mode which enables the machine to clean itself. The flashback machine comes alive again making a very loud noise as if someone fitted a van engine in the machine. With the loud noises coming from the flashback machine, Jason starts to pick up the cleaning tube and inserts it in the machine for the dust, that had been gathered up inside the flashback machine to come out. As the dust comes racing out, the room filled with air-dust which then led Jason to start coughing. As he coughed his lungs out, Jason quickly covered his whole face with a cloth facing it towards the window and then he opens it freeing the dust from prison.

After the craziness in the room, Jason

begins to remove the cloth from his face, which felt like he was in a desert surviving a sandstorm. Jason becomes relieved and says to himself " I never want to experience that again ". Jason cleans the left over dust from his face and then begins to check on the flashback machine. The flashback machine seemed to be finished with itself cleaning and then states " remove pipe ". As the flashback machine commanded Jason to remove the pipe, he quickly removes it and then places it in the equipment draw. Before leaving, Jason realises that he needs to leave the flashback machine on standby mode to save power so it dont start to blow stuff out of proportion which he then quickly leaves it on the mode and then starts to head towards meeting the group.

Chapter 12

New Life; New Me

Ana walks downstairs but stops half-

way and admires her happy family right
before her eyes. Her husband George sat
at the kitchen table sorting through some
of his work stuff, three happy children playing on the floor in front of the fireplace
together. Ana smiled to herself and carried on walking the rest of the way down
the stairs. She walks over to her children
and sits in front of the fireplace and begins
to play with them. George looks over and
smiles in content at the sight before him,
his beloved wife sat in front of the glowing
fire with his three perfect children, was a
sight he never wanted to forget. After a
while Ana got up off the floor and joined
her husband in the kitchen and started
cooking their tea. When the food was ready
Ana dished it up onto big platters and
placed them on the table and called the

children to go upstairs wash their hands
and take a place at the table. The small
family sat and ate tea together and they
all helped to clean the dishes and put them
away, and got the table ready for a family
game night. The three children were excited for game night they began running
around the house finding all the games that
they wanted to play and took them back
to the table and laid them out on the table ready to be played with. During the
games Ana sits back and looks at her little family and thinks to to herself, "how
can I be so lucky to have such a beautiful
loving family like this?" Ana just smiles
and continues playing games until it was
time to bath the children and put them
into bed.

Ana woke up one morning and smiled in

content at her new life and all that she had accomplished. Everyday Ana thinks about her old life and the people who she loved dearly and wishes that she could be back with them but on this one day Ana didn't think about her old life she was happy with this new life she is living now. Her children keep her going each day and she gets to see them grow up more and more each day and that makes her happy as they show her how much value she now has. Ana thinks to herself "I am the luckiest girl i know. My life has purpose, I have the perfect little family and a perfect husband. I couldn't ask for anything better than this."

Ana starts to think about her old life that she had to leave behind thanks to Jordan and his anger. She begins to think about all the things she missed out on for example her family and friends and all the special occasions like birthdays and Christmas. Ana then realises she can't let Jordan get away with all that he has put her through and how much her life has changed because of his thoughtless actions up on that cliff on that day. Once Ana has taken care of the children and her husband had gone to work she sits down at the kitchen table and starts thinking how she could get a message to her friends in the future and tell them where she is and what happened the day she ended up in 1837. Ana sits for hours just thinking about ways she could contact people of the future when suddenly, she had an idea. She said to herself, "I'm going to make a time capsule." Ana runs upstairs and into the children's room looking for a average sized box which she could use which will be suitable to withstand years of change and weather conditions. Ana finds the perfect box, she empties it out of the few bits that it's in there and takes it downstairs and gets to work on starting her capsule.

Ana looks around the house to find small things which she can put into the box to show her friends and family what she has managed to do with her new life and all the things that she has accomplished over the years. She puts in old paintings of her, George and the children, small things she has collected over the years, some of the drawings and bits that the children have made her so her family and friends can see how creative her children are. Ana also puts in the only thing that she has left

from her old life a silver engraved necklace
that her mother had given her for her 18th
birthday, which read "Happy 18th birthday my little angel, love you lots Mum X"

Chapter 13

Return of the Mac

After Mac brought his drink, decided to run back to his office despite him wearing his jeans and a sweatshirt he gets there

without any issues from his clothes restrict-
ing him. He gets to the street to where his
office is and he begins to slows his pace so
he doesn't tire himself out and this gives
him time to think through about how he
wants to word his story relating to the disappearance of Ana because he needs to
word it so he can get people's attention
and attract people who will want help Natasha
and friends to continue searching for Ana.

Soon as Mac enters his office, he throws
his drink onto the countertop and begins
to pace about to try think how he wants to
start this piece regarding about Ana and
how she disappeared and then it comes to
him that he needs to print out the photo of
Ana so he can keep his head on the topic
and not drift away like he did the morning which was silly of him to of drifted

away, daydreaming but if he didn't waste his morning away he wouldn't of gotten the chance to speak to Natasha and hear about this story. So he's glad that he wasted his morning away just to have this opportunity to be the person who has his name on this by line where it will actually be a helpful piece on his website.

Finally Mac sits down on his chair and begins to load up his website onto his post section and while the website is loading he places the picture of Ana near his computer so he can look at it for details of the disappearing girl and then he begins to start typing of what he knows already relating to the disappearance and how this girl who had her focus on her career completely disappeared without a trace or without anyone knowing how she has gone missing, Mac starts to type away with speed of a cheetah on the keyboard trying to get this piece out as quick as possible.

As Mac is typing away like his life depends on it, during is mad typing he begins to wonder about what to type next since he's typed all that he knows and now is just staring at the photo wondering what else he can add to the story to make it more interesting. Nothing comes to him so he just begins to space out and stare at the photo hoping for a another piece of information to come to him but nothing is coming, so Mac begins to just let his mind wander thinking about the various things he's seen throughout the day and wonder if he would of seen/hear the things he has done today.

Mac begins to just think how could of

a girl disappear without anyone knowing, just seems simply impossible, since it seemed like Ana ran the perfect life without any bumps within her life she seemed to be normal on all fronts so what was the thing thing what caused her to disappear without a trace. Mac begins to wonder about if Ana had any family members who knew about her disappearance.

Chapter 14

Swift and Reliable

The round begins and his boxing match

is off, as Jason proceeds to circle his opponent looking for a opening in their stance to strike at Jason begins to pace faster to see if it will make his opponent shift his stance to match up with Jason's which it works and as soon as Jason sees the opening he starts to make work of it and begins swing hooks and jabs at his opponent as often as he could at his opponents ribs and then proceeds to do a uppercut on his opponent and soon as it connected his opponent went flying across the ring from the sheer power of the uppercut and the ref runs over to check if the opponent is still breathing which he is just knocked out cold.

The Ref calls for the match to end in KO and proclaims Jason as the winner which then Jason celebrates in the ring before he heads back to the locker room to rest after his bout in the ring and wonders what he will do next since he's not scheduled to have another match for another month which frees up his time quite a lot so he wonders if he should begin to work on his machine again, soon as he thought this he decided to get dressed back into his clothes and leave the locker room to return home to think what else to do next.

Jason decides to contact the people who are searching for Ana, as soon he gets home he does that and asks if he can help with a machine he's built which allows him to look back into moments of the past and future. This will help them since it will allow them to get an idea what happened on the day of her disappearance which will give a clue to where they can look or who

they can question to find out more answers
towards the disappearance, after deciding
where to meet up Jason ends the call and
the proceeds to start to get his gear together.

Jason then continues to get his gear together and begins to wonder about if this
will be his big breakthrough if the group
take Jason up on his offer of using his machine and if they do and it works perfectly
then it will be a big breakthrough that
one of his machines worked and it will just
make Jason so happy to finally have a use
for his machine, and so he finishes packing
up and then proceeds to head out of his
house and just leave the house to meet up
with the group to see if they will take his
help.

Chapter 15

Blast from the Past

Hope begins to fill the air, the birds

are starting to sing their cheerful whistling song the group gather up with little to none doubt that they'll find their beloved friend Ana, they come up with plans on how they can find her but Jordan is just sitting there feeling sorry for himself, secretly laughing at how foolish the group are.

But then out of nowhere like an eagle swooping down from its prey Jason comes up with an idea about using his flashback machine to figure out what exactly happens to Ana on the day before and when she disappeared from the face of the earth. The response was unexpected because the group had laughed at Jason saying that "that's just impossible and stop making jokes".

Feeling confident in himself Jason proceeds to tell the group how this could solve the mystery about Ana disappearing, that they can pinpoint who has seen what before Ana went from the face of the earth. To create a picture like art being put together to figure out what had happened to their beloved friend.

He then carries on to tell the group how exactly the machine will work, that one person must sit onto a chair while wearing a type of head machine which he calls the Brain Buzzer while all the messy and complicated work gets left to him. Jason proceeds to try to persuade the group and says "we never know until we tried this, please can we just give it a shot".

With constant attempts of persuasion, trying to encourage the group it's worth a shot he decides to ask the group about what they think about the situation. Feeling depressed and worried Jason curiously waits for the groups response. The group begins to look at one another then back at Jason and it turns into an awkward deathly silence.

After three minutes of silence the group looks at one another again the group begins to laugh like a response from a comedian telling a funny joke. Jason left feeling humbled and upset that the group doesn't believe him start to have a small tear showing from his eyes, Jordan then steps up and says to Jason "don't be an idiot, that's impossible, they haven't even invented flying cars yet so don't be pathetic". The group then agrees with Jordans response which leaves Jason in tears because no one believes him.

Chapter 16

Discovery of Truth

Jordan decides it's worth to investigate

Jason's garage to be sure there isn't a flashback machine sitting there. In a heavy shock, like a hit to the back to the future film Jordan's eyes sparkle up to the sight of the time machine which Jason has built from scratch.

In fear Jordan falls to his knees, knowing that if he doesn't' do anything the group will find out what he had done to Ana. He starts to show signs of aggression like a lion fearlessly roaring to scare off his prey decides to constantly bang his head on the wall, nearly cutting his head open but proceeds that wasn't enough so he hits his hands on the wall.

Then in hopes of it just being a dream decides to try out if the machine actually works, as a result gave Jordan flashbacks to his childhood, how he was born

with paranoid schizophrenia but was un-
detected due to lack of Hospital resources.
How his Mother passed away at the age of
three and how is Father always used to
come back home drunk and abuse him,
physically hitting him and the constant
abusive language.

With images flashing like a picture being taken on a flashing camera the flash
backs carry on and Jordan is clutching on
to his seat. He then starts to remember
how he killed his father at the age of eleven
and starts to laugh at the flashback, then
images of Ana played, how he saw her watching him play for football in a hometown
match. The laughter starts to quickly turn
into painful tears.

Before going outside, Jordan drinks some
alcohol out of Jason's fridge to try and

calm his nerves....

Trying to regain his nerves and clear is head Jordan decides that he can't let the others know about it working, he tells himself even though the group knows that the machine is a load of bull Jason still may have a way to persuade them. In fear of him finally being caught he goes back into the flashback machine to remember on old friends name which he knew from prison and rehab.

Jordan knows the guys name which is John Kennedy, which by the Police is known as the Baba Yaga the Boogeyman who is the meanest and professional hitman in history but does not really remember his contact details which John gave him in rehab, so without second guessing Jordan uses the machine to remember what it was.

After receiving the number of the Hit-man Jordan is second guessing whether he should do this to Jason who is an old friend of his, with voices starting to speak inside Jordan's head like a deathly howling from a werewolf screaming furiously at the full moon he decides it's needed. That Jason must die to stop this situation from getting any worse, with no more doubt and a evil grin Jordan rings up John and arranges a hit on both Jason and his flashback machine.

With the weather taking a dark and tragic turn, the birds fleeing from the sky and a quick stroke of lightning coming from a sky like a bolt of death Jordan continues to arrange the plans with John about how he'd like Jason to die. With his voice turning evil like a deathly hallow and his hands twitching furiously he ends the call with the hitman and decides to walk out like nothing has happened.

Jordan is smirking and laughing because now he knows his finally off the hook once both Jason and his time machine is dead. He knows there is nothing stopping him and nothing can go wrong.

Not long now...

Chapter 17

Time Distorted

While Mac was letting his mind drift, he begins to remember about his desk and how messy it has become over the last couple days of him not doing any work, from being out of stories of what he could possibly write about. So Mac begins to start looking through his desk and notices that he's got some books left on his desk from doing some of his hobbies, which is looking into the history of different time periods and he begins to think about his favourite time period which is the Victorian era.

Mac begins to look through the books left on his desk and notices that one of them has a piece a paper sticking out, as a bookmark which he doesn't remember being there. So Mac investigates this page and he notices its relating to the Victorian time period just by the text and pictures of the page, where the bookmark is at, he now remembers why this page was marked due to unique likeness to the area he lives in and it looks similar but differently named to what it is called where he lives but that's what makes this unique.

As Mac starts to look through the book he starts to think about this will be a good story to write one day whenever he gets his breakthrough story, it won't matter what he will write about due to everyone will continue to read everything he will do once he makes it big so for now, he will continue to read through this Victorian book and then get some motivation and crack on with writing the piece on the disappearing girl. Shouldn't take Mac any longer since he can't find or think of anything else to put into the story.

While going through this book Mac begins to notice several pictures of a girl who looks completely out of the time period so then he double checks the photo to make sure it's not been tampered with or anything. He continues to keep looking for pictures of this strange girl throughout the books and he begins to notice a pattern throughout the book, it begins to be noticeable around certain areas what are close to where Mac actually lives and this begins to make Mac wonder, if he's spotted something changed with history and so he continues looking through this time period for any more pictures.

During Mac's searches through all of the books looking for pictures related to this girl Mac begins to spot several strange things with each picture the girl is involved in, and begins to spot in each picture it looks like she's wearing a digital watch, which is highly not possible since they weren't invented around that time period. Whatever this was it surely isn't possible surely these photos have had to be tampered with to show such an item within a picture relating to this time period so this picture must be genuinely, just means that this picture is completely real and not a fake...

Chapter 18

The Investigation

Natasha had booked the morning off
work so made the decision to do a little
bit of investigating into the disappearance

of her friend by herself because she knows quite a bit about crime herself being a lawyer and felt like from the knowledge she has she could help in some way. She then goes on to do some research on the case by herself while the rest of the group were busy working.

About 1 hour later she's left shocked that from the research she has done she can't find any information giving an idea into where Ana might be or what happened to their friend that day. The only information she was able to find then was the fact that they were no signs of any injuries. Natasha then began to think if there were any other ways to get some information on what might've happened as she was very desperate to get the answers she needed for her friend. Natasha felt that she couldn't rest until she knew exactly where Ana was.

After spending the next 15 minutes debating what to next she decided to see if she could find any witnesses that might've seen what occurred that day at the coast when Ana just disappeared into thin air without any trace of where she could be or if she was even still alive. Unfortunately, she couldn't find any witnesses that saw anything that day at the coast which really devastated her because she really felt like she didn't no if she could do anything else to figure out where their friend is because she'd already tried all the ideas she had and none of them lead to anything.

Natasha, shortly after deciding to stop investigating because she can't find anything else decides to print some of the very small pieces of information she managed to get so that she has them if she ever need to show them to anyone so that whoever she shows the to will be made aware that there isn't anything on where their friend Ana could be or what happened to her that day when Joshua decided to take Ana to the coast where she went missing.

After spending the morning carrying out her little investigation into the mysterious disappearance of her friends Ana, Natasha starts to pack away all of the information she had collected because she had to go to work for the afternoon but she would make sure that she showed her friends when she next saw them so they were aware of what she had found as soon as she next saw them.

Chapter 19

Murderous Intent

With the sun starting to settle, like a

helium balloon setting itself on fire and the sky starting to turn dark and dull, the hitman arrives at Jason's home, knocking on the door furiously like death coming through the door. Jason calmly opens the door to what he thought was the Police but to his surprise was a dark, demon eyed, scarred face, hair which blows with the wind, the man's name is known as John Kennedy.Jason tries to close it but to the surprise of the dark assassin kicking in the door nearly taking it off its hinges stops him.

The trained killer starts to attack Jason, throwing him on the table and giving him deathly blows to Jason's stomach and face, nearly breaking his nose. Then he is thrown into the TV which nearly sends Jason into a deep concusion. Glass break-

ing everywhere the hired killer continues
to dominate Jason and aims to give him a
slow death.

With blood pouring from Jason's head,
with ribs which are certainly broken tries
to find an opening so that he can protect
himself from the furious killer. With a
desperate blow the the assassins face Jason begins to defend himself. Only to be
stopped with a devastating kick to the side
of the head, constantly going in and out
of consciousness Jason is still desperately
trying to defend himself which isn't any
match for the trained, bloody killer.

With time drawing to an end with Jason, the killer finally gets his knife and
starts to stab Jason in the legs and slash
him on the back. The painful screams
could be heard from a block away followed

by a great but lifeless call for help, Jason is slowly passing out by the huge sight of blood going everywhere. A huge bang hits outside followed by a frightening roar rain starts to hit the floor like hail. Even the weather knows that this is going to be the end of Jason.

But suddenly Natasha and Mac charge in, attacking the assassin to stop him from killing their friend. Luckily the friends made it to Jason's aid just in time if they were a second later Jason would surely be dead, Natasha calls up an ambulance and quickly gets Jason to hospital.

Mac mutters to himself "this isn't over, am going to find who did this".....

Chapter 20

The Flashback

About 24 hours after first seeing the flashback machine and not wanting to use it because they all had concerns about what might happen whilst in the past. They are eventually convinced to use it, later on that day as Jason said to Natasha and the group "this is the only way that they will get the truth about what happened the day when Jordan took Ana to the coast where she was last seen." They were both worried about going to use the machine because of what they might see while they're in there. Also, because they are going to have to watch what happened to their friend.

A few hours later after being convinced to use the flashback machine. Jason takes the group back to the place where he is storing the flashback machine he made. They were all still quite nervous about what they were about to do, they were worried but just wanted to know the truth and had just accepted that this was the only way that they would get the truth because they weren't getting it anywhere else.

Still very worried the group make it to the day where they are wanting to see. They are preparing themselves for what they might see as it might shock them, they are secretly hoping she's fine and that she found somewhere safe but won't really know until they've seen the flashbacks. They then begin to see the flashbacks.

Flashback

'YOU ARE JUST FULL OF LIES!!" ' I KNOW YOU HAVE BEEN SEEING SOMEONE ELSE BEHIND MY BACK!! I HAVE SEEN THE MESSAGES ANA, I HAVE READ THE MESSAGES ANA, DON'T LIE TO ME!!" Ana just stood there expressionless and looks at Jordan unsure of what to say to him.

Jordan starts moving towards Ana causing her to move further back closer and closer to the edge of the cliff. Ana finds her voice and starts arguing back at Jordan. ' THE MESSAGES WERE A JOKE, THEY AREN'T WHAT YOU THINK THEY ARE ABOUT!! YOU SHOULD BELIEVE ME JORDAN I AM YOUR GIRLFRIEND!!" Jordan couldn't take no more of Ana's lies and pushed her, causing Ana to stumble and fall backwards over the cliff.

End of flashback

They finish watching the flashback where they then just stand there with tears streaming down their faces in silence and complete disbelief. They began to understand what they'd just seen, there friend being pushed off the cliff after getting into a fight when being confronted about the affair she'd had. They were annoyed that Jordan had been lying to them about what had happened since the day Ana had vanished without a trace.

They make it back in the flashback machine to the present day where they realise that they need to decide what they need to do about what they had just seen. They were heartbroken that they had seen this happen to one of their friends and were shocked that the person who was responsible for it had been lying to them since Ana had gone missing and had made the group feel so sorry for him when he was searching for her like he had no idea where she was. They knew that all of what they'd just seen pointed directly at Jordan but they had to make a decision on how exactly they would prove he was the one who caused her to disappear without any evidence to be found around the area where she was last seen.

Chapter 21

The Confrontation

When Natasha and the rest of the group

have return to the present day from the flashback machine where they have just seen what Jordan did to their friend. They were in complete shock and can't even talk because are in disbelief. They made the decision to go straight to see Jordan and confront him about what they had just seen happen to Ana while in the flashback machine Jason had made.

When arriving at Jordan's house they had to spend 5 minutes of their time banging on the front door and windows while shouting him to let them into the house so that they could talk to him. He eventually let them into his house to talk to him but he sat in the corner of the room acting innocent and like he didn't have any idea what was going to be spoken about.

They all started asking Jordan questions. Natasha said to him "What did you do to Ana?" Then Jason while shouting in anger followed on with "We saw everything you did to Ana when we were in the flashback machine that Jason showed us earlier on. Please just tell us the truth now Jordan" Mac then went on to say "Give up this innocent act now we know the truth we just want to hear it from you yourself."

They then sat in silence for almost 10 minutes waiting very patiently but also slightly anxious about what Jordan would respond with when he eventually would talk. They didn't have any idea if he would tell them the truth or not so they were really scared about what they might be about to hear from him.

After waiting almost 20 minutes for Jordan to respond to what they had all said to him previously he finally spoke. The first thing that he said was "Are you be-ing serious, accusing me of something that you saw in a stupid little flashback, it's just one big joke." The group just looked at ea-chother unsure what to say because they were all shocked that he was still trying to get away with it even after everything he'd just been told about so they just all sat there waiting to see if anything else was going to be said after. He started speak-ing again about 5 minutes later but still didn't admit anything he just said "Haha, you really think this is going to go any-where? You have no evidence really, all you've got is what you saw in that stupid machine that is pointless! Nobody will be-lieve you." Then the group all had tears in their eyes and walked out shocked that he couldn't even tell them the truth about what he did even though he knew that they had seen it all what he had done to their friend Ana when they used the flashback machine to find out what happened earlier that day.

After Jordan had finished talking total lies to the group of friends they all had tears in their eyes as they walked out the house slamming the door behind them. They were all angry, shocked and confused that he wouldn't tell them the truth about what he did to their friend Ana knowing that they'd seen it all while they were in the flashback to the day when he pushed her. He just thought was one big joke and that it was funny to keep them suffering while he was playing the innocent victim whose girlfriend had vanished after he'd pushed her into the sea off the cliff edge. .

Chapter 22

Living in the Past

After Mac discovers about this strange

girl he decides to look away and then notices that this girl looks oddly like Ana
which then he realizes it is her. This ex-
plains a little about Ana disappearing since
her body never was discovered at all when
she went missing This could be the reason
why, Mac instantly goes to call Natasha
and tells her all about his findings and
relating to Ana's disappearance and after
he's finished explaining all about what he's
discovered, Natasha begins to think about
ringing up the others which then Natasha
gives one of the friend's phone numbers to
Mac to see if they can meet up.

The group decide to meet up at Natasha's
place and then when they all got to her
place they decide to listen out to what Mac
has discovered and they all are anxious to
what they are about to hear and none of

them know what to expect to hear from Mac and this gets worse with how quiet everyone is waiting for them to hear exactly what Mac has to say with them expecting the complete worst thing possible, Not knowing what to expect they are getting worried and afraid what they might hear some of them begin to get skittish.

Finally Mac lets out his discovery of Ana being in one of the Victorian books, Jason can't believe what he is seeing and Natasha is sitting there quietly trying to process it properly since Natasha she already know of the photos from the call but she was a bit sceptical regarding about it cause how was it possible that Ana who disappeared couldn't of suddenly appeared in a different year it's just impossible yet it seems somewhat unlikely but anything is possible. With this new found information it makes the group wonder if they have just bared witnessed to time traveling somehow and this makes the group curious of how Ana must of got sent back into time from her being disappeared.

With this new found information regarding Ana being in a different time period it seems very unlikely that they can't do anything else but explore about it to see if there is any way to guarantee where Ana is or if she actually has been displaced through time and that what's the curious part of these pictures is that how is it possible that Ana appears in them yet there is no way she's that old, it makes Mac wonder if there is a link between her sudden disappearance and how she's all of a sudden popped up within these books without an obvious connection. The group start to wonder if there is a possibility of it being a freak accident or blessing towards Ana since its allowed her to live her live out without the stress of the modern life.

Chapter 23

Dear Sammy

Ana finishes putting pieces into her time capsule but she feels like there is still something missing from it. Ana sits back down at the table and goes through what she already has in there to give her an idea of what she is missing. It then comes to her a letter. A letter telling everyone what happened and how they can catch Jordan in the act, and get justice for me. Ana gets up and goes to the draw where they keep all the writing materials and goes back and sits down and thinks about what she wants to write

Dear Sammy,

I know it's been a long time since we have spoken and actually seen each other but there's something I need to tell you and it's really important, I hope you take me seriously and do this one last thing for me.

As you may have noticed I haven't been around for a very long time and you probably haven't been able to find my body after the 'accident". Well I'm here in 1837 the Victorian era. Yes you read that correctly the Victorian era. I don't quite know how I got here but it is so much more different to modern day and it has taken a lot of adjusting and getting use to.

The truth is on the day of my disappearance Jordan found out that I had been having an affair behind his back and he didn't deal with it in a very humane manner. He messaged me that day asking me to meet him and we would go for a walk along the beach, so I met up with him at our favourite Cafe just down the road from the beach. I kind of knew there was something off when I met up with him he was acting shifty and he looked really anxious but I didn't think to much into it and carried on walking with him.

Once we reached the beach he stopped and asked me if I was having an affair, and me being me as you know I denied the whole thing and tried to convince him that i wasn't and I was saying everything I could so I could get him to believe me. But he got all up in my business screaming in my face that he knew I was lying and he knew the truth he had seen the messages.

Then that's when things went wrong and he started getting closer to me, causing me to walk backwards until I could no more. We reached the cliffs edge and he completely lost it and he pushed me, I stumbled backwards, lost i balance and i went over the edge of the cliff. Then it felt like forever after that happened I woke up here in 1837. I now have a family of my own and a loving husband who has been with me since literally day one.

I need you and everyone else to get justice for me and get Jordan sent down, I can't finish living my life knowing he got away with 'killing me". I need you to go to the cliff on Tuesday 12th June an hour before 13:20 and set up a video camera angled at the edge of the cliff. I need you to record my 'death" and take it to the police and show them what truly happened to me.

I'm counting on you Sammy please don't mess this up, Jordan needs to go away for this.

I miss you all loads I hope you are all well and have families of your own and you are all happy. I hope neither of you have forgotten me, I think of you all everyday.

I love you all. Here's some painting and things I have collected over the years which I thought you all might want to see and have a piece of me. I have also put in my silver necklace my mother got me this is so you know that it is truly me and I am truly reaching out to you.

Yours sincerely

Ana

P.s Good luck

Ana folds up her letter and puts it into the time capsule, closes the lid and takes it to where her old house in the future would be. Ana goes inside and makes her way up the stairs and hides the box in the dresser and then starts praying that Sammy and her friends will find it in the future.

Chapter 24

Lessons of Time

After finding out about Ana being displaced in time, the group begin to wonder if there is any possible way that Ana might of sent a message from the past and Mac begins to ask "if there was anything

that she might kept over all these years"
and Natasha replies " she use to wear a
Silver engraved necklace all the time due
to the last couple weeks she kept it away
in a little box" suddenly Natasha realises
that she could of left a message within the
box with the necklace as a way of showing
that it was truly her who wrote the note.
Jason asks Natasha " Do you know where
she kept that box?" Natasha replies " yeah
I do actually, she kept it in her bedroom,
maybe we can go retrieve it from the house
and see if anything changed inside the con-
tents of the box"

The group go to Ana's house and find
that it's empty due to no one being home.This
makes it easier for the group to get into the
house and get the box, to check for any
changes within the box. So they instantly

go towards Ana's bedroom and this where they find the box on it's dresser. Natasha grabs the box as she enters the room and begins to look into the box. They notice that the locket is there. They also notice that there is a piece of paper amongst other bits and pieces such as paintings and small objects.

During this Mac offers to read the note and he sees that the note had a name on the front. Mac asks "Who is Sammy?" Natasha replies saying "That is Ana's cousin, she doesn't live far from here. We probably should deliver the note to her since it's addressed to her". They all agree to go deliver the note to Sammy out of respect for Ana. They set off to where Sammy lives. They all grab their coats and take the box and they leave as quick as they can.

After deciding to deliver the note to Sammy they all agree that they shouldn't listen to what the note has to say, since it's not addressed to any of them other than Sammy, and it wouldn't be respectful of them. So that's what they all agree to do. When they get to Sammy's place. Natasha wonders how will Sammy take the note? Since it's a the last thing of what she has from Ana.

So they continued to walk towards Sammy's home and with hopes she is there to receive the message from Ana.

As they approach Sammy's place, Mac and Natasha begin to wonder if they will be able to go through with this due to having no knowledge of the note at all. So they wonder how will Sammy take the note since she was very close with Ana and it will probably be Ana's last wish which hopefully Sammy will do.

They finally reach Sammy's place they decide to knock on the door and wait to be answered. Sammy opens up the door and sees Natasha, Mac and Jason and says "Hello guys, how can I help you?" Natasha responds "well we just came by to drop of a note addressed to you from Ana which we discovered" Sammy responds " Oh okay" Sammy takes the note off Natasha. Natasha proceeds to say " well we only came to drop of the message have a nice day" and the group proceed to leave and Sammy is left standing there with the note which she proceeds to read..

Chapter 25

The Reveal

After receiving a strange note Sammy
felt that it is time to investigate what happened to Ana on the day of her disap-

pearance. She packed up her equipment that she needed and started to head to the coast. Full of thoughts she tried to remain calm and professional about the situation but she said to herself she's done this for ages so she has the experience and knows what to expect. But in this situation she is concerned she won't be making it back home.

When she arrived the weather took a drastic turn, it was like she was back in the past and that the area she was in was haunted by an unknown presence. Feeling nervous her hands began to shake but Sammy tried to calm herself down and unpack the equipment that she had brought with her.

While she set up on the cliff she heard a deathly whisper saying "help me" followed by a deafening scream, Sammy began to have small panic attacks but tried her best to ignore it and do what was needed to be done.

Not knowing what to expect Sammy saw two figures going towards the cliff, one matching Ana's description and the other matching Jordan's. By Ana's facial expressions seemed happy and was excited to be at this cliff as she knew it's near the beach but Jordan's was just dull, like he is about to lash out at someone as he had fire in his eyes. While walking towards the cliff Ana attempted to talk to Jordan but only received a blank response, then showed signs of no interest like something horribly wrong was about to happen like a lion preparing to pounce at it's prey.

Once they arrive Jordan asked about

the supposed affair that Ana had which suddenly caused Ana to change her facial expressions to shock and fear. She knew how Jordan can react over the smallest of things so she mutters to herself which wasn't loud enough for Sammy to hear.

Sammy feels as if she's saw enough but knows she had to carry on watching for Ana's sake. Then out of nowhere like a flash of lightning Jordan snaps at Ana, shouting at her and accused her of lying to him. As a result Sammy was shaken up and was worried about what's going to happen. Like a ghost tale which was once a romantic couple turned to ugly and evil.

Jordan snapped like a thick metal that's under a load of pressure and started walking closer and closer to Ana, which looks as if he was stalking his prey ready for the right moment to pounce. Ana moved back trying to avoid Jordan but ended up getting closer and closer to the end of the cliff. Jordan with evil in his eyes like the devil walking on earth carried on arguing with Ana and suddenly out of nowhere like a bullet being shot from a gun he pushed her off the cliff.

Sammy had quickly covers her eyes in the horrible shock of what just happened, she tried to remain calm and cover her ears so she can't hear the sound of the long deafening screams of Ana falling down and then it turned into silence. Sammy watched Jordan looking down off the cliff where Ana was falling then walked away to where he had just came from smiling.

In shock and disgust Sammy threw up all over the grass but she was proud that she's finally got enough evidence to put Jordan away for a long time. That finally Ana would get some justice once and for all.

Chapter 26

Justice To Be Served

Sammy has then successfully managed

to get a recording of the incident where Jordan pushes Ana off the cliff edge. She straight away rings Mac and Natasha making them both aware that she has managed to get the proof they need.

Sammy the goes straight to meet Natasha and Mac with the footage of proof of what really happened to Ana and whether or not it was Jordan who killed her. She then spends the next 10 minutes debating what will happen now i have the proof. Will Jordan be arrested?? Will he get away with it? There was so much confusion that she just wanted to get to Natasha and Mac as quickly as she could.

When Sammy arrives at Natasha's place she immediately passes the tape that the recorded footage is on to Mac and Natasha. They then proceed to watch it to see if it's enough proof to get Jordan arrested and sent to prison.

As soon as the tape had finished they both looked directly at each other in complete disbelief of what they had just witnessed. They were crying and then immediately decide to ring the police to inform them about the new discovery because they feel that it is the evidence the police need.

About 15 minutes after they rang the police they arrived to watch the footage that had been collected by Sammy earlier that day. After watching it and having a discussion with each other the police decided they had enough evidence to arrest Jordan and send him to prison for the rest of his life. After the police had left the group felt that justice had been served because they had found the evidence needed to get Jordan arrested.

Ana thought to herself that she didn't want to go back home in the future, even though she missed all of her family and friends she had a second chance at life and she was much more happy with her new life than she was with her old one, she didn't want to give that up. She had three perfect children and a loving husband that loved her dearly. Her old life was just one big mess she didn't have much happening for her and she didn't have a family of her own. That night Ana sat with her husband cuddled up watching her children play happily on the floor. Ana was happy. She had achieved so much. She was proud of all that she had accomplished. Ana would always remember her old life

and everyone in it, she would never forget any of them or any on the memories,
they would be treasured memories that she
would never let go of. Although Ana had
to make some big changes in her life to
be able to fit in and live her new life she
would never change any of it for the world.
She had the perfect little life and it was the
life she had always wanted even if it wasn't
in the time era she hoped it would be in,
it was still her perfect little family which
she adored. Ana's youngest child snapped
her out of her little thought bubble div-
ing on her to give her a hug and a kiss on
the cheek before climbing off of her and
running up the stairs to bed. Ana didn't
realise she had been in thought for as long
as she was. Ana didn't mind though her
memories made her happy and seeing her

little family together and grow together was just the best feeling. In away Ana was thankful for her second chance at a new life. She hated the thought that Jordan did what he did to her and completely turned her life upside-down and the thought she will never see the people she loved again. The thought of what her life could have been like if she hadn't travelled back in time scared her. But Ana quickly shook that thought from her head and focused on what was happening now. Ana walked up the stairs to check on the children and tuck them into bed, then got into bed herself and cuddled up to her husband and fell asleep happier than she had ever been before.

THE END

Our Authors

Ivo Parkes

My Hobbies consist of Reading and Gaming, listening to music and Magic The Gathering, I love spending time with family. I want to become a teacher as my aspiring job. I hope you will enjoy this book.

Paignton Smith

Hi, I love to spend lots of time with family and friends going out to parties and just exploring. I like to go on long walks either with people or on my own. My hobbies consists of drawing, listening to music (I have a varied music taste), going out with family and friends and generally going out exploring and travelling. I am currently studying travel and tourism and I am about to start applying for my second year. One day I hope to move abroad and maybe own my own business. I don't really read book and novels, or even write them so doing this is a completely new experience from me.

Simon Taylor

Hi, I love listening to Country Music and loves horse riding and doing country folk stuff. My biggest interest currently is the Police and I am looking forward to serving my country as a Police Officer. I am hoping to be doing Public Services for the next three years in high hopes that I'll reach my goal. I am not normally a person to write books or novels, normally the fella to sing along to Keith Whitley or do the craziest of things. Though it's odd living in a city as a Cowboy it's always interesting as everyday is a new day.

Ellie McPhilbin

Hi, I enjoy listening to music by Ariana Grande, Little Mix and spending time with my family and friends. I also enjoy going to parties where I can spend more time with my friends because we are able to catch up. I also love going away with my family where we can spend time together. I am currently on a Kick Start course at college which gaining workskills while i re-take my exams. Next year I am doing a travel and tourism course.

Israar Nasir

Hi, I am a person who loves to listen to a lot of music which includes American rap or UKrap or even hip hop music. My favourite singer would be 2pac as I enjoy listening to all of his music as they bring a lot of true and emotional lyrics about what's happening with the world. I am also very interested in watching combat sports such as boxing and I love Muhammad Ali as my favourite boxer. I am also currently studying business level 2 and hope to get onto level 3 for a 2 year course and then be qualified to get into Uni. I also like to spend time with my friends and family and enjoy doing stuff together. I am also not a big fan of reading novels or any sorts but this has been a good experience for me and enjoyed it.

20308790R00093

Printed in Great Britain
by Amazon